# AVEN GREEN

## SLEUTHING MACHINE

# AVEN GREEN

## SLEUTHING MACHINE

DUSTI BOWLING

illustrated by GINA PERRY

STERLING CHILDREN'S BOOKS
New York

**For Monet**

**STERLING CHILDREN'S BOOKS**
New York

An Imprint of Sterling Publishing Co., Inc.

ISBN 978-1-4549-4221-4
978-1-4549-4184-2 (e-book)

Distributed in Canada by Sterling Publishing Co., Inc.
c/o Canadian Manda Group, 664 Annette Street
Toronto, Ontario M6S 2C8, Canada
Distributed in the United Kingdom by GMC Distribution Services
Castle Place, 166 High Street, Lewes, East Sussex BN7 1XU, England
Distributed in Australia by NewSouth Books
University of New South Wales, Sydney, NSW 2052, Australia

For information about custom editions, special sales, and premium and corporate purchases,
please contact Sterling Special Sales at 800-805-5489 or specialsales@sterlingpublishing.com.

Manufactured in Canada
Lot #:
2  4  6  8  10  9  7  5  3  1
02/21

sterlingpublishing.com

Cover and interior design by Jo Obarowski

# Contents

# Chapter 1

# The Whole Truth

Most people don't realize it, but there are a lot of mysteries to solve in elementary school. I'm only in the third grade, but I've been solving mysteries for a really, really, *really* long time— one whole *month.*

And I don't solve mysteries like any old detective. Nope. You see, I don't have arms. Yep, you heard me. No arms here on my torso, which I'd like to add is already eight years old.

Here, I'll say it again, as you may not have understood me correctly, because most people don't have as many brain cells as I do: I don't have any arms or fingers or hands or elbows or forearms or biceps. I just have shoulders, but nothing under them.

You're probably wondering why I don't have arms. People are always curious where they went. Well, they weren't eaten off by iguanas in the Galapagos. Just try saying that ten times really fast: iguanas in the Galapagos, iguanas in the Galapagos. My tongue already got all twisted.

My arms weren't pulled off in a particularly ruthless game of tug of war. They weren't blown off by a firecracker, and they weren't flattened by a steamroller.

Nope. The truth is I was just born like this. I know, I know. Boring stuff. But that's the truth, the whole truth, and nothing but the truth, which my parents make me tell. Otherwise I would have told you a much more interesting story about how they got scrubbed off at the Kansas City Quick Car Wash.

Anyway, I've already solved many mysteries with my brain of many brain cells. In case you don't know what a brain cell is, it's like the building block of the brain. Really, cells are the building blocks of everything that's alive, but they're not rectangular. They're more like blobby circles so tiny you need a microscope to see them.

The very first mysteries I ever solved were *The Mystery of the Missing Ice Cream* and *The Mystery of the Sticky Floor*. Here's the story of those two: one day the mint chip ice cream went missing from the freezer. It simply disappeared like a disappearing magician or something!

There was nothing but a trail of melty, sticky green drops left behind. Mom and I followed the trail to the kitchen table, where there was still a big circle of melted green ice cream. I had a hunch that it came from a bowl. There was also a spoon left behind with sticky toe prints all over it. Mom and I followed the ice cream trail away from the kitchen table all the way to the trash can, where we found the empty ice cream box!

So mysteries are easy to solve when you're the culprit. In case you don't know what a *culprit* is, it's the person who did the crime. And then their parents make them do the time—the time-out, that is.

I then went on to solve *The Mystery of the Bad Breath* and *The Mystery of the Smelly Feet*. Those were pretty easy to solve, too. Just a little toothpaste and soap was all I needed.

Of course there are some cases even my brain of many brain cells can't solve. *The Mystery of the Cereal in My Underpants* is still unsolved to this very day.

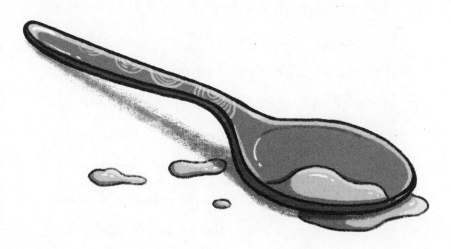

## Chapter 2

# Who, Why, Where, When, and What

I like to write down all the mysteries I solve, so I can keep track of them. I've solved so many at this point, Mom had to get me a new pack of paper to keep writing them down. She also helps me organize my mysteries into groups of *who, what, where, when*, and *why* mysteries.

A *who* case could also be called a *whodunit* case because it's all about *who's done it*. A good example of a *who* mystery I solved was *The Mystery of the Flower Drawings on Mom's*

*Romance Book.* That was an easy *whodunit* to solve. Why? 'Cause I dunnit, that's why.

A *why* mystery is when I try to find out *why* something is happening. A good *why* mystery I solved happened immediately after *The Mystery of the Flower Drawings on Mom's Romance Book.* I called it *The Mystery of the*

*Cranky Mom.* It's a *why* case because I thought to myself, "Why is Mom so cranky?" Then I thought to myself, "Oh yeah, because I drew flowers all over her book." I thought they really added to cover, but I didn't realize it was a library book.

By the way—in case you're wondering how a person without arms draws flowers on a romance book, let me tell you: They use their feet. Or at least I do. I can't speak for every person in the world who doesn't have arms, and there are a lot more of us than you realize. I suppose some people might use their mouths to draw flowers on a romance book. Or maybe they don't ever draw flowers on a romance book and then their moms are never cranky.

Another good *why* mystery I solved was *The Mystery of Why Valerie Gave Me Winter Gloves for My Birthday.* The answer to that one is that Valerie doesn't have as many brain cells as I do.

Not all of my mysteries are so easy to solve, though. A good *where* mystery I solved was *The Mystery of Emily's Missing Glue Stick.* Only I could find that missing glue stick. I found it right under Emily's butt.

A *when* mystery is when I try to figure out when something happened or when something is going to happen. A *when* mystery I try to solve pretty much every day is *The Mystery of When I'm Going to Get My Dessert*.

The last type of mystery I try to solve is the hardest. These are the *what* mysteries. I call them *what* mysteries because when I try to solve them I ask myself, "What in the world is going on?" A good *what* mystery I solved was *The Mystery of the Poop in the Middle of My Bedroom Floor*. It ended up being just a candy bar, not poop, which meant it also solved the daily *Mystery of When I'm Going to Get My Dessert*. That one was really tough. And tasty.

# Chapter 3

# P.I. Job Requirements

I'm so good at solving mysteries that Mom and Dad have even called me a private investigator, or P.I., for short. I've looked up what it takes to become a P.I., and it's very hard. One thing that's helpful if you want to be a P.I. is being able to speak multiple languages. I can already speak four.

Okay, I can already speak *parts* of four languages.

I can speak English: Long Live the Queen!

I can speak some Spanish: Uno, dos, tres, and all the way up to diez.

I can speak some French: Oui! Bonjour! Eiffel Tower! French bread! French toast! French fries!

I can speak some pirate: *Arrr*, mihardies!

Another thing that's helpful for being a P.I. is having a really good memory, so you can remember important facts and your P.I. kit (which every serious P.I. should have) and also when it's time to eat dessert.

But the thing that's probably the most help-ful of all things is having a super-powered brain full of lots of extra brain cells. In case you're wondering why I have so many extra brain cells, I think I've solved that mystery, too: *The Mystery of Why I Have So Many Extra Brain Cells.* Here's what I think: All of the cells that were supposed to make my arms went into making my brain instead. Two arms are a lot bigger than a brain, so it's amazing that my brain hasn't burst right through my skull.

And this wasn't in any of the requirements I've read about, but I would just like to add that a P.I. should probably take at least one bath every week. Remember, it's P.I., not P.U. Also, a P.I. should definitely be potty-trained. Because it's P.I., not Pee Pants.

But you know one thing I've never read as being necessary to be a good P.I.? Having arms. That's what.

## Chapter 4

# Not a Trace Left Behind

So one day I was just sitting at my school desk, turning the pages of my science book with my toes, learning all about how polar bears and penguins live on two different sides of the earth (mind blown!), when my teacher, Ms. Luna, announced it was time for us all to get ready to go to lunch. Then she let out a blood-curdling scream! Well, maybe it was more like a small shriek. Or a very loud gasp.

Okay, she really just clucked her tongue.

I closed my book and looked up at her. "Someone took my lunch," she said.

"When?" I asked, my P.I. brain of power already in full motion.

"While we were at the media center," she said. "They took all of it, even my new lunch bag."

"Not a trace left behind," I added, pursing my lips.

Ms. Luna nodded in agreement. "Not that I can see." She peeked under her desk like she thought her lunch bag might be playing hide-and-seek with her. She stood back up. "Nada. It's totally gone."

I glanced around suspiciously at my class-mates. Kayla, my best friend, looked at me, her brown eyes big and surprised. Emily, my other best friend, had her unibrow raised in a show of great excitement. I loved Emily's unibrow.

It was like a cute fluffy brown caterpillar crawling right across her big forehead. I was so excited that Kayla and Emily were coming to my house on Friday after school. We were planning on painting each other's toenails and having a full-blown Ninja competition and eating boxed macaroni and cheese for dinner because Mom always saves the best dinners for my special guests and—

I shook my head and turned my attention back to Ms. Luna. A P.I. never allows herself to get too distracted, even when the most exciting sleepover of all time is coming up.

Unfortunately, I didn't have my P.I. kit with me, so I couldn't dust for fingerprints. I glanced around the room at my classmates. "Reveal yourself, culprit!" I called out. I squinted at Robert. If anyone was capable of stealing Ms. Luna's lunch, it was Robert. He gave me a dirty look but didn't say anything. Everyone else stayed quiet, too, so my first strategy to reveal the criminal failed.

Ms. Luna's mouth dropped open. "Oh," she gasped. "I hate to think that it was one of you."

"Maybe it was Aven Mean Green!" Robert yelled.

I was most certainly not Aven Mean Green. I was nice to *everyone*.

"The only one who's mean around here is you!" I called back at him.

"You smell like toads!" Robert yelled back.

"I don't even know what toads smell like!" I said, though I was still really mad about what he said. "And you be quiet when you're talking to me!" I told him.

Ms. Luna raised her hands. "That's enough, you two."

If it wasn't Robert who'd stolen the lunch,

then this was going to be a tough *who* case. I would certainly bring my P.I. kit to school tomorrow so I could figure out *The Mystery of Who Stole Ms. Luna's Lunch and Brand-New Lunch Bag Because, P.S., It Wasn't Robert.* Maybe I'd shorten that mystery name.

Ms. Luna told us all to line up for lunch, so I put my science book away and slipped my tie-dyed flats on. I always wore flats because they were easy to slip on and off. I had six pairs: tie-dyed, sparkles, smiley faces, kitties, purple, and plain old white (*booooring*).

We all lined up at the door. "But what are you going to eat?" I asked Ms. Luna.

She sighed. "I guess I'll have to eat cafeteria food today."

"Well, lucky for you, today is chicken nugget day," Emily said. "They're shaped like dinosaurs, too."

Ms. Luna wrinkled her nose. "Lucky me indeed."

Then we all marched in a line toward the smelly cafeteria. We were surprised at what we saw as we walked up to the counter to get our nuggets. Cafeteria workers waved their hands in the air as they spoke to each other. Apparently, not only had someone stolen Ms. Luna's lunch, they'd also stolen an entire bag of sandwich bread, leaving only the ripped-open bag and some bread crumbs behind.

"Just look at this disaster!" one of the workers declared. "Who would do such a thing?"

I stood up on my tiptoes so I could see inside the kitchen and scanned over the crummy mess. "Someone who is a very messy eater," I said. It looked even worse than under the kitchen table after I'd eaten a bowl of Cheerios. Mom always complained that I put nearly as many

Cheerios on the floor as in my belly, but she was wrong. There were usually *more* Cheerios on the floor than in my belly.

This couldn't be a coincidence. Someone stole Ms. Luna's lunch and brand-new lunch bag, and now someone had stolen a bag of bread from the cafeteria. I was sensing a pattern. I formed a *hypothesis* in my mind. A hypothesis is a really good guess about why

something's happening. And my hypothesis was that the same person had stolen the lunch bag and the bread, and they were probably still nearby.

*The Mystery of the School Food Thief* was going to be a tough mystery to solve, but if anyone could solve it, I could. Right after I finished my dinosaur-shaped chicken nuggets.

## Chapter 5

# King Smith of Kansas City

After school, I sat down to work in my P.I. office, which is located on top of the middle couch cushion in our living room. I was doing some important research, which may or may not include watching episodes of *Scooby-Doo*, when Mom came in with a sad look on her face.

My brain went over all the things I could have done wrong that day.

Drawing on one of her books? Nope.

Eating candy before dinner? Possibly.

Forgetting to flush the toilet? Probably. Leaving grimy footprints on the couch? Absolutely, though it was really hard to tell which ones were new.

Mom flopped down on the couch with a sigh. "King Smith of Kansas City is missing."

I jumped up. "Oh no!" King Smith of Kansas City wasn't really a king; he was my great-grandma's dog, which was even *worse* than if an actual king were missing. We usually called him Smitty for short, but I could tell this was a highly serious situation, and in highly serious situations, it is always best to use full *legal* names. Legal means it's not against the law, so I could use full legal names all I wanted.

I sat back down next to her and immediately got to work. I picked up my pencil with my toes and positioned a paper on the coffee table. "Where was he last seen, Laura Green?"

I asked my mom. Like I said, full legal names.

"She let him out yesterday morning, and he never came back."

I wrote all of this *pertinent* information down. In case you don't know what pertinent means, it basically just means important. I think one day someone must have been eating a very large donut, and they meant to say important, but it came out all muffled and a new word was created. Like this one time, I was eating a large donut, and I tried to say "delicious," but instead it just came out "gugushus." As far as I know, gugushus has not been added to the dictionary yet.

But like I said, a P.I. never gets distracted, so moving back to King Smith of Kansas City, which was the pertinent issue. "Which door did she let him out of?" I asked. "Front or back?"

She frowned. "I didn't think to ask her that."

I nodded. "Of course you didn't. Only real P.I.s think of the pertinent questions." I set my pencil down and stood up. "You better take me over there. I'll need to investigate while there's still time."

## Chapter 6

# Mrs. Great-
# Grandma Mabel Jackson

Mom dropped me off at Grandma's trailer and left to run some errands, which was good. I didn't need her messing up the crime scene with all her fingerprints.

I sat down on the ugly green couch with Grandma, who had her face scrunched up extra wrinkly today. "I just don't know why he'd run off like that," she said, her voice all quivery. "He's never done this before."

I picked up the pad and pencil with my feet

and set them on the coffee table. "Now, Mrs. Great-Grandma Mabel Jackson, if that is your real name, I have some very important questions for you."

She nodded. "Shoot."

I cleared my throat. "Are there any dessert foods on these premises?"

She frowned. "Yes. Do you think that has something to do with his disappearance?"

I narrowed my eyes at her. "That depends. What sort of dessert foods do you have on these premises?" *These premises* is a really official way to talk about a place, and I liked to be as official as possible while working.

Grandma removed her thick glasses and cleaned them with her polka-dot blouse. "Well, I think I have some banana bread."

"You'd better bring it out here immediately," I said. "It could be good bait for King

Smith of Kansas City. And if that doesn't work, it will be good brain fuel for me." Lots of brain cells means lots of extra brain fuel is needed to keep them happy.

I watched Grandma slice some banana bread in the kitchen while I sat on the couch pondering the pertinent information I had so far:

1. **King Smith of Kansas City had never run away before.**

2. **Grandma didn't know why he would run away.**

3. **Grandma only had banana bread for dessert, which was not the best.**

4. **I needed to remind Grandma to buy some mint chocolate chip ice cream.**

Grandma set the banana bread on the coffee table and sat back down. I wiped my feet with a baby butt wipe then grabbed a chunk of banana bread with my toes and popped it into my mouth. There was still plenty for Smitty.

"Now," I said through my bite, then swallowed. "Did you hear anything weird before King Smith of Kansas City disappeared?"

"Like what, honey?" she asked.

"Like a loud roar or a person saying 'Here, doggy-doggy' or a very loud siren?" I didn't bother asking Grandma if she *saw* anything because her glasses were as thick as the banana bread she had just sliced.

Grandma shook her head. "Nope. Nothing like that."

I nodded thoughtfully. "That's good."

"Why is it good?"

"Because now we know that he wasn't eaten by a roaring predator or dognapped or sucked up by a tornado."

Grandma smiled. "That is good." Then her

big old eyes got even bigger. "Maybe it was the government," she whispered.

I nodded. "I think that is a very good hypothesis."

Suddenly there was a loud engine sound outside. I jumped up and looked out the little

trailer window. "Who's that?" I asked about the man riding around on a great big lawnmower near Grandma's yard. Grandma sighed. "Oh, that's Ralph. He just moved in next door."

"Has he been riding around on that lawn-mower a lot?"

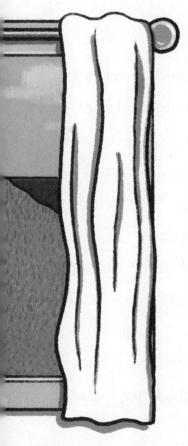

Grandma gasped. "Oh yes, he has. Do you think that scared Smitty away?"

Actually, I was just think-ing that riding around on a lawnmower was probably lots of fun, and I was hop-ing he might let me drive it. But what Grandma said was much better.

I turned to her. "I think it is *very* likely."

# Chapter 7

# Fresh Dog Hair

I got the fingerprint powder and duster out of my P.I. kit. One day my mom dropped her face powder on the bathroom floor and it busted all up into little pieces and she said a word I'm totally not allowed to ever say. So she let me use it for my fingerprint powder.

"Where did you last see him?" I asked Grandma as I dusted the doggy door. It's always important to ask where someone was last seen. For example, if they were last seen in a kitchen eating a bowl of spaghetti, then we might be looking for a trail of noodles. Or if they were last seen in a swimming pool, then we might be looking for water puddles and a wet person.

"He ran out of here to go relieve himself and never came back."

I dropped the duster from my toes and stood up. "We'd better head outside then, if that really was the last place he was seen."

"Well, I guess I didn't actually see him out there. I just saw him go out."

I pondered this information. "I think since you saw him go outside, we can assume that's where he went, even if you never saw him out there. Is there anywhere else he could go on the other side of this door besides outside?" This case was getting complicated.

Grandma shook her head. "No. No, I don't believe so."

"Okay, good." I footed the duster to Grandma so she could carry it outside for me, and we headed to where King Smith of Kansas City was last assumed to be, which was on the other side of the doggy door.

I immediately found more evidence in the form of dog prints on the porch. I dusted them.

"Do you really need to dust them, honey?" Grandma asked. "I mean, we can see the prints already."

"I am always thorough," I told her, even though what I really wanted to say was *Don't tell me how to do my job, lady*, which I would never say because I had respect for extra-old people. And regular old people. And all kinds of grown-ups.

"I can really see where they're headed now," I said as I stood back up. "Let's follow them."

Unfortunately the prints ended when the porch did, but I kept going in the direction I thought they were headed, which was to Grandma's next-door neighbor Lou-Ann.

On our way over there, I saw something suspicious on the ground, and I bent down to take a look at it. "Hand me my magnifying glass, please," I said to Grandma, and she did as ordered.

I held it between my toes as I studied the hair on the ground. "Yep. Just as I suspected— dog hair. I believe we're on the right track."

"But couldn't that hair be from anytime?"

"No, it looks fresh."

"How can you tell that, honey?"

"Just trust me. I'm a dog hair expert. Please give me my special pen." Grandma once more did as ordered. My special pen was just the greatest gift I'd ever gotten in my whole life— it had a secret recorder on it. Emily had given it to me for my birthday.

The only problem was that it was really hard for me to turn it on because the buttons were tiny and obviously made for small fingers and not fat toes. And Grandma couldn't turn it on because she kept pushing the wrong buttons. But if we had been able to turn it on, I would have recorded my finding about the prints and the dog hair.

# Chapter 8

# Alleged Poop

We headed to Lou-Ann's house, and Grandma knocked on the front door. As soon as Lou-Ann opened the door, her face lit up. I had that effect on people. "Hello, Aven," Lou-Ann said. "What a nice surprise."

I gave her a serious look for this serious situation. There wasn't time for a bunch of chitchat. "Please take this pen and record our conversation," I said to her. She took the pen from me, but looked all confused. "It's a super high-tech spy pen," I explained. "You have to push the record button."

She did as told, and I dove into my questioning. "Lou-Ann . . . " I realized I didn't know her full name. "Lou-Ann of Cedar Springs Trailer Park, next-door neighbor to Great-Grandma Mabel Jackson, when was the last time you saw King Smith of Kansas City?"

"Oh, why? Is he missing?" Lou-Ann asked.

"Please just answer the question," I said. "The pen only records for like one minute." I tapped my foot on the front porch. "We've already wasted like half of that."

Lou-Ann scratched at her short curly hair. I sighed. More time-wasting. "I think I saw him yesterday."

"Where was that?"

"Out in the yard. He did his business—"

"You mean the business of pooping?" I asked. It's always important to be completely clear when investigating. Who knows what kind of business a dog might do? Digging, running around in circles, squirrel chasing, and barking were all dog business.

She nodded. "Yes. He relieved himself."

"Where is this *alleged* poop?" I asked. It's important to use the word *alleged* a lot when investigating. I think it means something might be pretend.

Grandma frowned. "I don't think that's probably important, Aven."

"You never know what might be important until you find it," I told her, and I thought that was a really smart thing to say, but unfortunately the pen had run out of recording room.

Lou-Ann walked us over to where she thought she'd seen King Smith of Kansas City poop, but I didn't think her memory was so good because there was no poop there. We walked around in circles until we found what looked like an approximately day-old poop.

I asked Grandma to open my P.I. kit. I removed my compass. I imagined a line from Grandma's front porch to the poop and adjusted my compass on the grass with my toes to see what direction that line headed in. "*Hmm.*" I said. "I believe King Smith of Kansas City was heading south."

We walked that way, and every now and then I would use my magnifying glass to check for hair and prints. "I found one!" I said, pointing my foot at the dog print in the middle of the field behind Grandma's trailer. I dug around in my P.I. kit and took out a small yellow flag. Lou-Ann stuck it in

the ground for me, and once more I took out my compass, which showed us we were still moving south.

We kept walking until we hit the street on the other side of the field. I looked all around, but we didn't see anything else—no more paw prints or hair or anything. We had walked so far that I could see my school down the road. "Bummer," I mumbled.

"It's okay, honey," Grandma said sadly while Lou-Ann patted her on the back.

But it most certainly was not okay. I had to find Smitty, and I had to find him soon. What if he was in danger? What if he was hungry? What if he needed to relieve himself and there was nowhere to do so? Would he explode?

I felt like I might explode right then and there, so we had to say goodbye to Lou-Ann and head back to Grandma's trailer. By the time I was done doing *my* business, Mom had returned.

"Any luck?" she asked.

"We found some prints and dog hair and poop, but no Smitty," I told her.

She frowned. "I'm sure he'll turn up."

But what if he didn't turn up? What if he turned down? I knew this would be the most important *where* mystery I ever had to solve: *The Mystery of the Missing Smitty.*

# Chapter 9

# Eyebrows

There was another ruckus at school the next day when the food thief struck again. This time, the victim was Mr. Collins and the birthday cake the other teachers had brought in for him.

Ms. Luna told us all about it. "You should see the mess!" she declared. "Strawberry cake everywhere. This wasn't just about stealing cake. This was a deliberate disaster."

I nodded. "We have a real criminal on our hands. A food destroyer."

Ms. Luna put her hands on her hips. "I think you're right, Aven. This person is quite a mischief maker."

"Can I go take a look in this *alleged* teacher's lounge?" I asked. I was pretty sure the teacher's lounge is *alleged* because I'd never even seen it before.

Ms. Luna frowned. "Students really aren't allowed in there."

"How on earth am I supposed to solve this case if I'm not even allowed at the crime scene?"

"I think they've already cleaned it up," Ms. Luna said. "So I'm not sure there would be much to investigate anyway."

"Of course they did." I harumphed. "Amateurs." An *amateur* is someone who does *not* know what they're doing.

I pondered the pertinent information I had so far about the school food thief:

1. They had stolen Ms. Luna's new lunch bag.

2. They had stolen a bag of bread.

3. They had stolen a whole birthday cake.

4. They were very, very messy.

5. Robert was giving me the stink eye, so he was still a suspect. But he was also a student, which meant he wasn't allowed in the alleged teacher's lounge. This case was getting complicated.

6. I was surrounded by amateurs.

7. My brain already needed a break from this case, and I couldn't wait for my sleepover with Emily and Kayla.

Just then, a woman walked into the classroom with a girl. The girl had long dark hair pulled back in a braid and wore a beautiful pink dress. Ms. Luna smiled and announced, "Class, this is Sujata. She's joining us for the rest of the school year. Isn't that great? Say welcome to Sujata."

"Welcome, Sujata!" I shouted, and I felt like I said it the most enthusiastically of everyone in the whole class. Sujata looked up at me, smiled a little, then looked back down at her pink shoes. Then Ms. Luna led her to an empty desk, and she sat down and all the excitement was already over.

I looked over at Emily and smiled. She raised her unibrow and smiled. Then she lifted up her backpack and patted it, and I thought, *Yes, I know you have your sleepover stuff in your backpack.* Then she opened

it and pulled out a stuffed koala bear. She waggled her unibrow at me. I waggled my eyebrows back and thought, *Yes, I know we're going to play stuffy salon.*

Then I looked at Kayla and she narrowed her eyebrows at me and made a chopping motion with her hand. I narrowed my eyebrows right back at her and thought, *Yes, I know we're going to have a Ninja competition.* The three of us had a whole conversation with almost just our eyebrows. That's how good friends we were.

Then I looked over at the new girl, Sujata, and saw that she was watching us. Then she looked away really quickly. And I noticed that *her* eyebrows looked really, really sad, but I didn't know why. I thought maybe I should work on solving *The Mystery of the New Girl Sujata's Sad Eyebrows*. Then again, I was overwhelmed with cases at the moment.

# Chapter 10

# Rainbow Barf

"We're going on a sleepover! We're going on a sleepover!" Emily, Kayla, and I sang on the bus after school. We were beautiful singers, even if Emily got a little shrieky at times.

The bus dropped us off in front of my house, and we ran inside. "After-school snack! After-school snack!" we sang, because after-school snacks were the most delicious of all foods.

"Goodness," Mom said. "Go right ahead. Just nothing too sugary." Then she left the room to fold laundry.

We pulled out a container of mint chocolate ice cream and mixed in a bag of gummy
bears and sprayed some whipped cream on
top. Because "nothing too sugary" is a matter of opinion. But we were only able to eat
about half of it before Emily barfed. What a
*lightweight*. A lightweight is someone with a
wimpy stomach.

Mom ran into the kitchen, saw our snack all over the kitchen table and the rainbow barf all over the floor, and gave me an angry look. "But nothing too sugary is a matter of opinion," I mumbled.

☆

"Ninja hand chop!" Kayla shouted, bringing her hand down on the stack of pillows in the middle of my bedroom.

"Ninja chin chop!" I cried, smashing my face against the pillows.

"Ninja elbow chop!" Emily elbowed the pillows, but not nearly as well as I chinned them. Plus she ripped a huge one, and Kayla and I couldn't stop laughing. "You guys, it's not funny! My stomach still feels gross."

"Ninja foot chop!" Kayla said, kicking the pillows across the room so we had to restack them.

"Ninja butt chop!" I hollered, jumping up and coming down hard on the stack on my butt. Then I toppled over onto the carpet, because it's harder to keep your balance without arms.

"Boy, I'm tired," Emily said, wiping the sweat from her forehead. "I don't think I can do another chop."

"Me too," I said, still lying with my face in the carpet.

"Sooooo?" Kayla said.

Now was the tough part—deciding who won the Ninja competition. We took it very seriously. Emily broke out the whiteboard and marker. Then she wrote our names at the top and made three columns. "Ten points for my elbow chop," she said, all braggy. Like it's so impressive that she has elbows.

"Ten points for my hand chop," Kayla said, and I had to roll my eyes.

"Ten *thousand* points for my chin chop," I said, but they scrunched up their noses at me, so I said, "Fine. Fifteen points."

"Fine then," Emily said. "Five bonus points for my toot."

"Why?" Kayla asked.

Emily squinted at her. "Distraction."

I actually thought Emily could've given herself at least ten bonus points for that, but I didn't say anything. Because I wanted to win, of course!

"Ten points for my foot chop," Kayla said.

"Minus five points for messing up the pillows," Emily said.

"One million points for my butt chop!" I cried.

She wrote the points down. Then she said, "Minus one million points for falling off the pillows during your butt chop."

I shrugged. She was always fair. We added up the points. It was a tie. I jumped up from the floor. "Good competition. Let's get some lemonade."

But Mom would only let us drink lemonade without sugar, which is really just lemon water, because she said we didn't need any more sugar. But that was really just her opinion.

# Chapter 11

# Robot Chickens

The next thing we did was paint our toenails. Emily chose a boring pink and Kayla chose silver, but I painted mine a beautiful sparkly purple.

"How do you like that new girl, Sujata?" I asked them while we painted our toenails.

Emily shrugged. "I don't know. She seems nice, I guess. I liked her pink dress."

"She has really long hair," Kayla said.

"She looked sad in class today," I said. "I wonder why."

"Maybe her hen droids are acting up," Emily said.

I frowned. "What's that mean?"

She shrugged. "I don't know. But whenever my grandpa looks sad, and I ask him about it, he tells me his hen droids are acting up."

"Hen droids?" I said. "Sounds like something from Star Wars—like chicken robots."

Kayla's eyes got huge. "Oh my gosh! Does your grandpa have chicken robots?"

"I don't know," Emily said, but I could tell she was as excited as we were at the thought.

"You should definitely ask him to explain exactly what his hen droids are next time you see him," I said.

This was a very interesting *what* mystery: *The Mystery of Emily's Grandpa's Hen Droids.*

Then we did another Ninja competition because we needed a tiebreaker, of course. But we smeared our nails everywhere and Mom had to change all the pillowcases. And she sighed a lot. And our nails were ruined.

We were already totally pooped by the time we sat down for dinner. Dad came in from work and kissed Mom's cheek. Then he looked down into the pot she was mixing and frowned, though I don't know why because boxed macaroni and cheese is the best dinner of all time!

Dad gave me a kiss on top of my head. "Hey there, Sheebs."

In case you're wondering why my dad calls me the silly name *Sheebs*, it's because when my parents adopted me at two years old, I acted like a queen needing to be waited on *foot and foot.* That's because my foster family had done everything for me. And Dad kept saying, "She thinks she's the Queen of Sheba!" I didn't need to be waited on *foot and foot* anymore, but he still called me Sheebs.

"You girls having a fun time?" Dad asked.

"Oh yeah!" Kayla exclaimed. "We've already had two Ninja competitions and we painted our toenails and we had an after-school snack."

Mom rolled her eyes and mumbled something about our after-school snack.

"Then I barfed," Emily said.

"Oh no," Dad said. "Are you okay?"

"Yeah, I feel great!" said Emily.

"You should have seen it, Dad!" I said.

"She barfed a rainbow that smelled like chocolate-dipped Fruit Loops!"

"Yes, it was lovely," Mom muttered.

Dad covered his mouth and did some gagging before leaving the kitchen.

When we all sat down to dinner together the doorbell rang. And it was Grandma!

She walked in all sadly and slumped down at the kitchen table with us. "Smitty is still missing, and I just don't know what to do."

"Did you check under your coffee table?" Emily asked, and I thought that was a very

good question. I hadn't even once thought to look under Grandma's coffee table.

"Yes, honey," Grandma said. "He's not there."

"Did you check under the bed?" Kayla asked. Wow. Maybe Emily and Kayla should've been the private investigators.

"Yes, dear," Grandma said.

"Did you check under the fridge?" Emily asked, and I decided maybe she wouldn't make a very good private investigator after all.

Grandma sighed. "I don't think Smitty would fit under there, but good thinking."

"Hey, you know what!" I said. "We should put up some missing dog posters tomorrow!"

Everyone at the table nodded. "That's a great idea, Sheebs," Dad said.

He should've known by now that I was chock-full of great ideas. "By the way," I said. "Emily's grandpa says his hen droids are

**67**

acting up. Do you think he has some kind of chicken robots?"

Grandma snorted a little and covered her mouth with her hand. "You mean hemorrhoids, honey?"

"Oh yeah!" Emily said. "That's it! That's what my grandpa has!"

But we never did find out exactly what they were because Dad choked on his macaroni and cheese and Mom giggled, and Grandma just said, "The bane of my existence," which I think means they're really bad, so I hoped Sujata didn't have them after all.

And I was *really* disappointed to find out that Emily's grandpa didn't actually have any robot chickens.

# Chapter 12

## All Worn Out

Luckily, we had lots of pictures of Smitty to choose from, and Dad designed a fantastic poster. We printed about a hundred of those bad boys, then we all went out that morning after breakfast (frozen waffles because Mom is the coolest!) to put them up around Grandma's neighborhood. We even put one on the school, which made me feel kind of important. I could just imagine everyone walking in and seeing the poster, and I would be like, "Yes, I know this famous missing dog."

I couldn't reach high enough to staple the posters to the poles and walls with my toes, so Mom let me *dictate* where they would go. I think I'm a very good dictator, and Mom and Dad agree. Emily and Kayla weren't as impressed with my dictating skills and insisted on putting the posters where they wanted.

A couple of times, we had to stop to give Grandma hugs because she started sniffling a bit. You see, Smitty was her best friend, and so we just had to find him because a great-grandma without a best friend was simply the saddest thing I'd ever heard of.

After all one hundred posters were hung, Kayla and Emily went home. That night dinner felt very sad without Grandma and Emily and Kayla there. And of course Mom didn't make anything as special as boxed macaroni and cheese—just stewed pot roast with lots

of vegetables and baked rolls and a side salad.
Side salads were only okay as long as I could
pour ranch dressing on them—just like half
a bottle.

We all chewed our pot roast more sadly
than we ever had before. "What if we don't
find him?" I asked.

Dad reached over and squeezed my shoulder, and I noticed he had some pot roast gravy on his chin, but I felt too sad to even laugh about it. "Don't give up hope, Sheebs. Hey, put that amazing brain of many brain cells to work. What should we do next?"

But my brain of many brain cells just fell back in my chair. "I think they're all worn out," I mumbled.

"Never!" Dad said. "They just need a good rest. I bet you girls didn't sleep as much as you should've last night."

"I heard them up giggling at nearly midnight," said Mom, giving me the stink eye.

"We wanted to see if we could stay up all night long," I said.

"And did you?" asked Dad.

"No," I said. "We conked out." And I felt like I was about to conk out right then and there at the table. And I almost did! And Mom told me to get my butt to bed. So I did. And then they tucked me in and said, "Good night, sweet Sheebs," which always made me feel warm and fuzzy. I would think about Smitty tomorrow.

## Chapter 13

# Sves the Swedish Dognapper

I went back to Grandma's the next day after church because it was Sunday. And Dad was right. My brain cells felt good and rested after sleeping for about a hundred hours straight.

Mom dropped me off so she could go grocery shopping, and Grandma and I sat on the couch. I broke out my magnifying glass and cleared my throat. "We've looked outside," I said. "But we haven't really looked inside yet."

Grandma sighed. "I know he's not in here, sweetie."

"Of course I know that, Grandma! I just mean maybe there are some clues inside about where Smitty might have gone."

"If you think so," said Grandma.

"First we should look in the freezer," I said. So we did. I saw there was mint chip in there and I ate a bowl, and Grandma got some good Grandma points for that.

Now that my brain cells were adequately fed, I told Grandma to take my notebook, and I picked up the magnifying glass between my chin and shoulder and headed toward Grandma's bedroom. I dropped the magnifying glass on the floor, then held it between my toes and studied the carpet. It was pretty dirty.

"Dirty carpet," I told Grandma. "Please write that down."

Grandma frowned, but when I gave her a serious look, she started writing in my notebook. "I just don't know why *that* would be helpful," she mumbled.

"You don't know what might be helpful until you find it." I looked under Grandma's bed and saw a ball under there. I kicked it out. "What's this? Is this Smitty's toy?"

Grandma shrugged. "I don't think so."

It had letters on it. "S–V–E–S," I said. "Who's Sves? He sounds *Swedish*." I waited for Grandma to look impressed that I said such a smart thing, but she just looked puzzled. "Like a Swedish artist," I added. "Or a Swedish teacher. Or a Swedish handyman."

"I don't know any Swedish people," Grandma said.

"I think this guy Sves might be the clue to finding out where Smitty is. Like maybe he dognapped him." I thought a moment. "Sves the Swedish Dognapper," I whispered to myself.

It sounded about right. This Sves could have lured Smitty with this ball, then grabbed him, dropping the ball at the same time.

"I don't know, honey," Grandma said. "Maybe it means something else."

But I really liked my new hypothesis. And lucky for me, old people still had phone books. "Grandma, where's that giant phone book of yours that everyone else throws in the recycling except you?"

We went to the phone book. The names were in order of last name, so I tried to find someone with the last name of Sves. I remembered how things are alphabetized from school. I finally found the name of Svart and laughed, but Grandma didn't get the

joke. I ran my toe down the listings. "Sverdbeev, Sverdlove." I snickered. These names were *awe-some.* My last name seemed really boring all of a sudden. "Sverkos, Sverner, Svesko, Svetan." I frowned. "Oh no. I passed it. And there was no Sves. And I can't possibly read all the first names to find him."

"Maybe he's just not in there," Grandma said.

But I knew this Sves was lurking around somewhere. Probably close, too. Just waiting to jump out at us from behind any corner. My eyes darted around the trailer. *You won't get the better of me, Sves*, I thought. *Oh no, you won't!*

# Chapter 14

# Acronyms and Other Revelations

I kept thinking about Sves while I was at school the next day—did he have a skinny mustache that curled at the ends? I could see him twisting his pointy mustache in evil ways while he lured Smitty out of the house with that ball, cackling the whole time. I told Mom my hypothesis, and she said maybe we should cut down on the *Scooby-Doo,* but I had no idea what that had to do with Sves and his evil mustache.

I was thinking about Sves so hard that when my teacher called on me, I didn't know what she was even talking about. "Please repeat your question," I said.

"Aven," she said. "I asked what seven times nine is." She pointed at the problem on the board.

"How can you expect me to think about times tables when an evil dude named Sves has dognapped Smitty?" I cried, slumping down at my desk.

She looked very confused. "Sves?"

"Yes. We saw his name printed on the ball he dropped

when he stole Smitty. We're pretty certain he used the ball to lure Smitty, just like you'd use a worm to lure a big old bluegill."

She smiled. "How do you spell that?"

"S-V-E-S of course." *Sheesh*. You'd think teachers would know how to spell simple words like Sves.

"You mean like 'Sunrise View Elementary School?'" she asked.

How could she not know that S-V-E-S did not spell that? First of all, it was way too short.

"No. That would be spelled S-U-N-R-I-S-E-V—"

"Aven," she interrupted me. "I know how to spell the school name. I'm saying that S-V-E-S could be an *acronym* for our school."

"What's an acronym?"

Just then, that new girl, Sujata, raised her hand. "It's the first letter of each word in a name," she said softly.

"Good, Sujata," Ms. Luna said. Then she wrote the word on the board. "It's when you take the first letter of each word in a name and put them together."

"Oh, I get it," I said. "A.L.G. is my acronym."

"Yes," said Ms. Luna. "Except we call those initials."

"Because English is *tricky*," I said.

Ms. Luna laughed. "Yes, it is sometimes," she said. "Here is another example of an acronym." She wrote *U.S.A.* on the board. "This is the acronym for the United States of America."

"But shouldn't it be T.U.S.O.A.?" I asked.

"Well," she said, rubbing at her forehead, leaving a big chalk splotch on it. "Sometimes we leave out the unimportant words."

I shrugged. "I think 'the' is a pretty important word, if you know what I mean. I would never say, 'I need to go bathroom.' Because then I would sound like a big baby."

"Anyway," she sighed. "S.V.E.S. is the acronym for our school. And we write that on a lot of things. And doesn't your grandma live right up the street?"

I stared at her. "What are you saying exactly?"

"I'm saying, Aven, that the ball probably came from the school and not from some dognapper named Sves."

I jumped up so quickly that I knocked my chair over. "Oh my gosh! Someone from our school dognapped Smitty!"

Ms. Luna did not think that anyone from the school had dognapped Smitty. "But what about all the crime around here lately?" I said. "This school is riddled with crime!"

I thought about Ms. Luna's missing lunch and brand-new lunch bag. I thought about the mess in the cafeteria. I thought about the big cake disaster. And that ball—SVES. The paw prints and path of poop leading so far across the field behind Grandma's trailer. And, of course, Smitty loved to eat cake, bread, and bagged lunches. I felt like some new hypothesis was forming in my mind, but I couldn't quite put my toe on it.

I slipped off my glittery ballet flat and dug around in my bag with my foot until I found my magnifying glass and recording pen. Good thing I'd brought them today. I'd had a feeling I might need them.

"Ms. Luna," I said politely. "Can we take a class trip to the alleged teacher's lounge?"

"What for, Aven?"

I held up the magnifying glass in my toes.

"Clues about the food thief."

"Students really aren't allowed in there."

"But this could be the big break I've been waiting for," I said.

Ms. Luna sighed. "How about if I check in there later during lunch?"

"But you're not a highly trained private investigator," I said.

"Oh, I'm very good at observation," said Ms. Luna. "If there's anything in there, I'll find it."

But I had my doubts. Ms. Luna didn't even see Robert picking his nose and flicking his boogers at Kayla right as she was bragging about her observational skills!

# Chapter 15

## Group Work

"Time for history," Ms. Luna announced. "Let's get to work on our new group projects. We're going to break up into groups of five, and each group is going to pick a country for a report and presentation."

And can you believe it? I got to be in a group with Emily and Kayla! And that new girl, Sujata, joined us. And then Ms. Luna said the worst thing ever when she told us, "I'm sure you girls won't mind Robert joining your group."

I absolutely did mind, but I didn't say so because Mom always told me I didn't have to say absolutely *everything* that went on in my head. The problem was it was just so hard to keep it stuffed in there.

Everyone broke up into groups. The moment we sat down together in one corner of the room, Robert was already being a problem by looking at me and making toad noises. I'd have liked to shake my fist at him if I'd had one. Shaking your clenched foot at someone did *not* send the same message.

"So what country should we pick?" I asked because I am a natural-born leader, as Mom and Dad always said.

"How about Kansas?" Emily said.

"Emily, that's not even a country," I told her.

"Yeah, it's a city, dumb toad!" Robert said.

"It's a state," I corrected him.

"No, it's Kansas *City*," Robert said.

"Kansas City is a city," I said. "Kansas is a state."

Everyone looked confused already.

"How about India?" Sujata said, so softy we could barely hear her.

Robert rolled his eyes. "I've never even heard of Innie. Sounds like a belly button."

"She said India!" I told him, but I didn't add the words "stupid face" like I wanted to. I just kept that all stuffed inside my head where it belonged.

"I know a lot about India," said Sujata in her quiet voice. "My grandparents lived there. And we could make Indian food to bring in for everyone when we do our presentation."

"Awesome," I said. This Sujata was really smart. And what she said got me thinking about food because I was always hungry at school. Smitty was always hungry, too. And

the food thief seemed awfully hungry to steal so much food. And—

"I don't want to do India!" Robert cried, right as I was on the brink of a major revelation. I wanted to scream because I seriously could not work (or think!) with this boy.

Then our whole group erupted into shouting because of Robert.

Ms. Luna stomped over to our group. "What in the world is going on here?" she asked.

We all pointed at Robert.

"Out in the hallway now," Ms. Luna said. When we got out there, she peeked next door and asked the aide to come watch over her class. Our class shared an aide with the class next door, but we hardly ever saw the aide because that class next door must have been a real handful.

Once the aide was inside, Ms. Luna closed the door and stared down at us, arms crossed. "Now just what is the problem?"

I was clearly the leader of the group, so I spoke first. "We all want to do our project on India, but Robert won't agree, and this is all very frustrating because what I really want to do is go investigate the alleged teacher's lounge and not work on this project."

Ms. Luna tapped her foot. "Aven, I already told you I'll look in there later."

"But I need to look now! Right now!" I said.

"Why?"

"Because the evidence could be disappearing every single second we wait!"

"What evidence?" asked Ms. Luna.

"Food thief evidence!" I said.

Ms. Luna rubbed her forehead. She was doing that a lot today. "Okay, fine," she finally said. "If we take a quick trip to the teacher's lounge, will you let this go?"

I smiled and nodded. "I just need my magnifying glass and special spy pen."

## Chapter 16

# Strawberry Paw Print

Ms. Luna quietly got my magnifying glass and special pen from my desk, and the five of us made our way to the alleged teacher's lounge while the rest of the class worked on their projects. Suckers.

Ms. Luna peeked into the teacher's lounge, which was no longer alleged (because I was about to see it with my own two eyes), and no alleged teachers were in there messing up the crime scene. "All clear," she said, and we went inside.

This must have been what that astronaut dude Neil Armstrong felt like when he stepped on the moon for the first time. We all gazed around in wonder. There was a big long table with lots of chairs and a coffeemaker and a microwave and a fridge and (WHAT?!?) a box of donuts just sitting on the counter that still had little donut holes left in it!

I looked at Ms. Luna, then at the box of donut holes, then back at Ms. Luna. She shook her head at me. "We're just here to investigate, Aven," she said.

Ms. Luna held the magnifying glass and recording pen for me while I searched around where the cake had been. When I got to one corner of the room, I had her hand me the magnifying glass, and I studied

a leftover smear of chocolate frosting that had been missed. "*Aha!*" I said. "Please turn on the recording pen." Ms. Luna did as I asked, and I decided she was a fine assistant. I stood up and cleared my throat. "Paw print!"

Ms. Luna turned off the pen and got down to study the print. "Oh my goodness," she said and looked up at me. "You're right!"

Of course I was right! "I think we should visit the next crime scene," I said. "The cafeteria." And lucky for us, a new crime had just been committed that morning. All the lunch workers were breaking out brooms just as we walked in the door. "Stop!" I cried. They were going to sweep up all the evidence. *Amateurs.*

Ms. Luna walked behind me as I followed the trail of Tater Tots through the kitchen and out the doorway. Then down, down, down the stairs. All the way to another place we'd never been before—the basement!

Ms. Luna pushed on the door to the basement. "The lock is broken," she said. "Look at this." She pushed the door open and closed. Then we all entered the cold, dark basement.

Ms. Luna flipped a few switches before a bulb hanging from the ceiling finally came on. "Stay close," Ms. Luna whispered to all of us as we crept through the place, the one light bulb barely enough light to see anything very well.

There was lots of theater stuff, like the barn from the Old MacDonald play the kindergarten did. Boy, was that a baby play. And I knew because I was in it. I played a cow that went moo moo here and moo moo there.

We heard a scary creaking sound, and I shivered. *Creak, creak.* Someone whimpered. I think it was me, but I decided I would blame Robert if anyone said anything.

"Don't worry," Ms. Luna said. "That's just the radiator. It gets pretty cold down here."

"I wasn't worried," I said bravely. Then I gave Robert a look that said *Stop being such a baby.* He stuck his tongue out at me.

Sujata pointed a shaking finger at a shelf that was covered, simply covered, in chopped-off hairy heads. I gulped a gulp of fear.

"They're just wigs," said Ms. Luna.

I turned around
to look for Emily
and Kayla because
I was getting kind of
scared, and I watched in horror as Robert
grabbed a wig from the shelf and shoved
it right on Emily's head. "*Ahhhhhh!*" Emily
screamed. "It's got me!" She jumped around
in a circle, slapping at her head. "Get it off!"

Just then Sujata reached up and grabbed
the wig off Emily's head and threw it across
the basement, where it fell behind another
shelf. Ms. Luna walked to Emily, who was
now crying, and put an arm around her.
"Thanks, Sujata," Emily said through sobs.

Sujata smiled shyly down at the floor.
"You're welcome."

Then Ms. Luna gave Robert the evil eye.
"A letter will be going home today, Robert."

I snickered because a letter was just about the worst thing that could ever happen, and Robert deserved the worst.

We kept walking through the basement, Ms. Luna now holding Emily's and Sujata's hands. I pointed at a mysterious thing on a shelf. "What is that mysterious thing?" I asked.

"Oh," said Ms. Luna. "That's a typewriter."

"What's a typewriter?" asked Kayla.

"It was used to type papers. With ink," explained Ms. Luna.

"Who used it?" asked Emily, her voice still shaking.

"Cavemen," Robert whispered.

"No, not cavemen," said Ms. Luna. "It wasn't that long ago."

"Then why didn't they just use a computer?" asked Kayla.

"We didn't used to have computers," said Ms. Luna.

"Wow," said Robert. "You must be really, really old."

Ms. Luna frowned. "Let's move on, every-one," she said.

I pointed at a wooden paddle-looking thing with little holes in it. "What's that for?" I asked. "Looks like a wooden fly swatter."

"Oh my," said Ms. Luna, her hand going up to her cheek. "Well, that's, um . . . That's . . . "

"Spit it out, for goodness sake," said Robert.

"That's for spanking."

We all gasped. "Who gets spanked?" cried Kayla.

Ms. Luna shifted on her feet. "Well," she said. "When I was little, kids got spanked when they misbehaved in school."

"What in the world?" I cried. "Did you ever get spanked?"

Ms. Luna's brown cheeks had turned bright red. "Just once," she said.

"What did you do?" Emily asked.

"I think we should just keep moving," said Ms. Luna.

"Yeah," I said. "Good thing you're not allowed to get spanked anymore, right, Ms. Luna?"

"Actually," said Ms. Luna, "it's still legal here in Kansas, even though our school doesn't use it anymore."

"*Legal,*" Emily said. "What's that mean?"

"It means it's not against the law," said Ms. Luna. "It's still allowed."

"Spank Robert for what he just did to Emily!" said Kayla. "Spank him!"

Robert slapped his hands against his cheeks. "*Nooooo!*" he whined.

"No, Kayla," said Ms. Luna. "Moving on now, please." She gave us all a *look*.

That was too bad because Kayla was really on to something with this whole Robert getting spanked idea.

Suddenly, Emily screamed, "Dead body! Dead body!"

Ms. Luna grabbed the body from the corner. "It's just a CPR dummy."

Kayla frowned. "Dummy is not a nice word. My mom told me."

Ms. Luna dropped the dummy and held a hand to her chest. "I'm going to have a heart attack before we get out of here."

But this basement was the most exciting place I'd ever been in my whole life! Emily had gotten attacked by a hairy wig. And now I knew I could spank Robert if I wanted to because it was *legal*. And we found out that Ms.

Luna was so old she knew what a typewriter was. And now there was a dead dummy body!

I looked down and spotted a Tater Tot and remembered the whole reason we were down here in the first place. "This way," I whispered to everyone, and they tippy-toed quietly through the basement, the radiator creaking. Suddenly I stopped. "Who's whining?" I said. And I knew it wasn't me this time.

Ms. Luna looked around the group. "Is everyone okay?" she asked. Everyone did not look okay. Emily looked cold and shivering. Kayla's eyes were extra big. Sujata was sniffling.

"What was that?" Kayla whispered.

"Let's find out," I whispered back.

We followed the whining sound, winding our way around old computers and broken desks and cleaning supplies until we ran into a skeleton!

Everyone shrieked.

"It's a*liiiiiive!*" Robert shouted.

"No, it's not!" said Ms. Luna. "It's just for science class." She picked up its hand and jiggled it, making all the bones knock together. It whined again. Kayla dove behind a giant tower of baskets, Sujata covered her face with her hands, and Emily looked like she might faint.

Ms. Luna let go of the skeleton's hand and peeked around a bookshelf. She laughed. Then she looked at me and said, "Aven, come here."

I walked on shaky but strong legs to Ms. Luna.

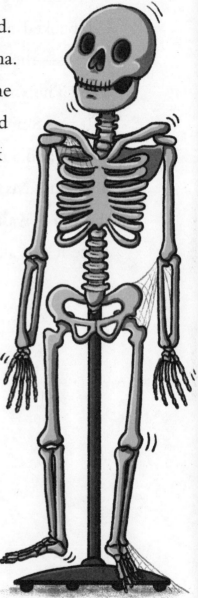

"Look," she said.

I peeked around the bookshelf, and there he was—the culprit! The criminal! The food thief! The whiner!

It was Smitty!

And also a mess of bread and cake and Tater Tots and Ms. Luna's brand-new lunch bag, though I wasn't sure she'd want it anymore since it was all smeared with Smitty's slobber.

# Chapter 17

# Celebration Dinner

That night, we were all so happy that we decided to have a celebration dinner with Grandma and Smitty and Emily and Kayla. And Mom made the most special dinner in the whole world—buttered noodles!

And guess what else? Sujata showed up! Turns out Sujata had been really sad since leaving her friends and family behind at the place she used to live—a very mysterious place called *Baltimore.*

After we found Smitty, and Grandma came

and picked him up and all the excitement died down, Kayla, Emily, and I asked Sujata to play with us at recess. Emily was so grateful to Sujata for saving her life from the hairy wig, and I thought Sujata had showed tremendous bravery down in the basement.

Then Sujata told us she'd been sad because she was lonely and she even cried a little, and I said, "I know how to solve that!" Then we all four played together at recess, and I invited her over to our house for dinner. So I had officially solved *The Mystery of the New Girl Sujata's Sad Eyebrows.* This was the busiest week ever.

Emily, Kayla, Sujata, and I sat on the living room floor petting Smitty. After he'd had a bath, of course. He'd been all covered in dust and peanut butter and spiderwebs from hiding down in the school basement.

"What if we'd found Smitty, and he was

wearing one of those wigs down there?" Kayla said. "Like a disguise?"

"Yeah, and what if we'd found Smitty," I said, "and he was using the typewriter to send secret letters, and it turned out he was a time-traveling spy dog from hundreds of years ago and that's why he knew how to even use a typewriter?"

Emily's eyes got huge. "What if we'd found Smitty, and he was eating a whole pile of Tater Tots?"

Sujata nodded quietly, and I sighed. "That's basically what really did happen, Emily." *Sheesh.* She really needed to work on her creativity skills.

Sujata didn't talk much yet, but that was okay. Because it's okay to be shy, of course! I was shy once. It was on a Wednesday afternoon in kindergarten.

Then we all ate dinner together and Mom surprised us with a special celebration cake that I helped her bake myself. It was the kind with carrots in it, but you can't taste the carrots at all, and that makes it taste extra good. I really loved helping Mom bake that cake.

But the best part of the night was when Grandma whispered to me, "It was all because of you, Aven. You're the best P.I. in the whole world."

And I knew she was right.

## Chapter 18

# Retirement

After dinner, my friends' parents came and picked them up, and we drove Grandma and Smitty home. When we got to Grandma's, we saw that her neighbor, Ralph, was out on his loud riding lawnmower. Smitty hunched down in the car and whined. "Yep," I said. "That definitely scared him."

Dad got out and asked Ralph if he could turn the lawnmower off. Then they talked a second, and Dad walked back to the car. "You can take him in now," said Dad. "And he'll make sure to warn you before he mows from now on, so you can keep an eye on Smitty."

"Wonderful," said Grandma. We all got out of the car and walked Grandma up to her trailer, then she gave me a little hug and went inside with Smitty.

"Come here, Aven," Dad said, putting his arm around me and walking me over to Ralph. "This is Mr. Pitt."

I giggled, and Mr. Pitt shrugged. "Yeah, when I was in school, they called me Ralph Armpit."

"I don't even have armpits," I said.

Ralph nodded and smiled. "So your Dad said you might like to try driving the lawnmower."

I looked up at Dad because *how did he know*?

He grinned down at me. "I know my Sheebs."

Mr. Pitt stepped down from the lawnmower

as I slipped off my flats. Then Dad helped me up on it and got on behind me. I gripped the steering wheel with my feet as Dad started the lawnmower back up. "How do you know how to work one of these things?" I asked Dad. All we had at home was a push mower.

"Oh, I know a lot of things," he said, and that made me laugh because he really didn't know that many things.

The sun was setting as I steered the lawn-mower around Mr. Pitt's and Grandma's yards, and Dad only had to grab the steering wheel every few seconds to put me "back on track." My heart was full of happiness knowing that Grandma and Smitty were inside the trailer together, safe and sound, while I got to drive the lawnmower.

On the way home, I let out a big sigh as I looked out the car window.

"What are you thinking about Aven Green Sleuthing Machine?" asked Mom.

"I'm thinking about retiring from the P.I. business," I said.

Mom and Dad were quiet a moment. "Retiring, huh?" said Dad. "Why's that?"

"Well, I just solved the biggest case I ever had. I feel like I should retire on a high note. Just like Grandma retired from the bread factory before that factory totally destroyed her back and when she was finally old enough for her penance."

Mom giggled. "*Pension*."

"I don't want to destroy my back either," I said. "And maybe I could get a pension, too."

"What were you thinking exactly?" asked Dad

"Fifty dollars per day."

"How about fifty *cents* per day?" said Dad.

"And only if you do all your chores," Mom added.

"Yes!" I cried. I was going to be rich.

"But what will you do now?" asked Mom.

I shrugged. "I don't know."

"Well, you know we believe you can do just about anything," said Mom.

"I know." I sighed. "The world is my toy store."

Mom giggled again. "You mean the world is your *oyster*," she said.

I frowned. "That doesn't make any sense. Why would I even want an oyster? Gross. I like what I said better."

"I think I do too, Sheebs," said Dad. "And the world really is your toy store."

"Yeah," I said. "Especially now that I get fifty cents every day!"

"What do you think you'll do with your new fortune?" asked Dad.

I thought a moment. "I really loved baking that carrot cake with Mom. Maybe I'll start a baking business."

"Oh," Mom said. "The fair is coming up, and they always have a baking contest."

"That's it!" I said. "Watch out, world! Here comes Aven Green Baking Machine!"

# Aven's Sleuthing Words

**Culprit:** the person who did the crime

**Hypothesis:** a really good guess based on evidence about why something happened

**Legal:** not against the law

**Pertinent:** having to do with the matter at hand (or, in my case, at foot)

**Premises:** a really official way to talk about a building and the land around it

 **Alleged:** something that might be pretend because there's no proof

**Amateur:** someone who does *not* know what they are doing; not a professional

**Acronym:** when you take the first letter of each word in a name or phrase and put them together

# Coming to a bookshelf near you
## in Fall 2021!

Aven Green knows she's an expert baker and a supertaster (someone with excellent taste buds). So she's certain that, with a little help from her friends, she can win a blue ribbon for baking at the county fair. But having  four people with different opinions in one kitchen ends up being a recipe for disaster.